10656953

This book belongs to

....

I celebrated World Book Day 2020
with this brilliant gift from my local
Bookseller and Puffin Books.

#ShareAStory

CELEBRATE STORIES. LOVE READING.

This book has been specially created and published to celebrate **World Book Day. World Book Day** is a charity funded by publishers and booksellers in the UK and Ireland. Our mission is to offer every child and young person the opportunity to read and love books by giving you the chance to have a book of your own. To find out more, and for loads of fun activities and reading recommendations to help you to keep reading, visit **worldbookday.com**

World Book Day in the UK and Ireland is also made possible by generous sponsorship from National Book Tokens and support from authors and illustrators.

World Book Day works in partnership with a number of charities, who are all working to encourage a love of reading for pleasure.

The National Literacy Trust is an independent charity that encourages children and young people to enjoy reading. Just 10 minutes of reading every day can make a big difference to how well you do at school and to how successful you could be in life. **literacytrust.org.uk**

The Reading Agency inspires people of all ages and backgrounds to read for pleasure and empowerment. They run the Summer Reading Challenge in partnership with libraries; they also support reading groups in schools and libraries all year round. Find out more and join your local library. **summerreadingchallenge.org.uk**

BookTrust is the UK's largest children's reading charity. Each year they reach 3.4 million children across the UK with books, resources and support to help develop a love of reading. **booktrust.org.uk**

World Book Day also facilitates fundraising for:

Book Aid International, an international book donation and library development charity. Every year, they provide one million books to libraries and schools in communities where children would otherwise have little or no opportunity to read. **bookaid.org**

Read for Good, who motivate children in schools to read for fun through its sponsored read, which thousands of schools run on World Book Day and throughout the year. The money raised provides new books and resident storytellers in all the children's hospitals in the UK. **readforgood.org**

PUFFIN BOOKS

THE CASE OF THE DROWNED PEARL

PUFFIN BOOKS

UK | USA | Canada | Ireland | Australia
India | New Zealand | South Africa

Puffin Books is part of the Penguin Random House group of companies
whose addresses can be found at global.penguinrandomhouse.com.

www.penguin.co.uk
www.puffin.co.uk
www.ladybird.co.uk

First published 2020

001

Set in 11/16 pt New Baskerville Std
Typeset by Jouve (UK), Milton Keynes
Printed and bound in Great Britain by Clays Ltd, Elcograf S.p.A.

A CIP catalogue record for this book is available from the British Library

ISBN: 978–0–241–42731–6

All correspondence to:
Puffin Books
Penguin Random House Children's
80 Strand, London WC2R 0RL

MIX
Paper from
responsible sources
FSC
www.fsc.org FSC® C018179

Penguin Random House is committed to a
sustainable future for our business, our readers
and our planet. This book is made from Forest
Stewardship Council® certified paper.

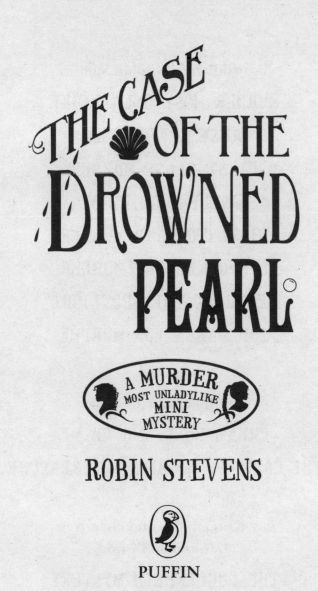

THE CASE OF THE OF THE DROWNED PEARL

A MURDER MOST UNLADYLIKE MINI MYSTERY

ROBIN STEVENS

PUFFIN

To my brother Richard and my sister Carey, who know what beaches are supposed to be like.

THE CASE OF THE DROWNED PEARL

Being an account of
The Body at the Seaside,
an investigation by the Wells and
Wong Detective Society, with assistance
from the Junior Pinkertons.

Written by Daisy Wells
(Detective Society President), aged 15,
and Hazel Wong
(Detective Society Vice-President and Secretary),
aged very nearly 15.

Wednesday 29th July 1936.

HAZEL

My name is Hazel Wong, and I never expected a murder on my summer holiday – but then nothing about the English seaside was as I'd imagined it.

Two and a half years ago I was sent from my home in Hong Kong to Deepdean School for Girls, a very English boarding school. Before I arrived, I hoped I might have polite English boarding-school adventures, with midnight feasts and jolly pranks, and a best friend who looked like a character from an English children's book. And I *did* – but somehow the midnight feasts and the pranks became the least exciting parts of my life in England. For my best friend Daisy Wells and I have been caught up in several real-life murder mysteries during the last few years, and we are now seasoned detectives, with horrid murders, kidnappings and midnight chases as ordinary to us as Geography lessons.

I am not the girl I was when I first arrived in England – but all the same she is still there, underneath everything that has happened, and some things never change. No matter how hard I try to understand the English, I never quite succeed. And this trip was no exception.

When Daisy and I were invited to the seaside by Daisy's mysterious Uncle Felix and Aunt Lucy, and instructed to bring our friends (and rival detectives) Alexander and George, I was delighted. A beach to me is a soft, smooth stretch of sand, between pure blue sea and high green mountains. The water, when you dip your toe into it, is as warm as a bath, and the sun beats down beautifully hot.

I know now that I ought to have been prepared. I have suffered through two chilblainy English winters, three blustery springs and three drizzly summers, but somehow I still saw that soft white beach in my mind.

And then we stepped off the train at Saltings

yesterday, and a seaweed-strong gust of wind slapped my face and rain spattered against my cheeks, and Daisy took in a huge breath and said, 'Oh, heaven!'

I stared at her in shock. My teeth were chattering and my bare legs were goosepimpled. This was not the beach holiday of my imagination. This was hardly a holiday at all. This was torture.

George burst out laughing at the look on my face, and I glared at him.

'Hurry up, all of you!' said Aunt Lucy briskly, leaning into the wind. 'The hotel's just down this street.'

She had on a very sensible tweed suit, and looked as dull and respectable as anything. She fitted in perfectly with the other cheerful English holidaymakers piling off the train, clutching buckets and spades and chattering – but I had the feeling that whatever mission she and Felix were on was not respectable in the slightest.

That, of course, was why the four of us were here: to pretend to be ordinary children on holiday while they carried out an important and secret errand for the government. Uncle Felix wiped drops of rain from his monocle, and winked at me.

'It ought to clear up soon,' he said.

But it did not.

Saltings was small, bare and white, the houses as flat and featureless as the sky. We arrived at our hotel in another terrific gust of rain. The sea was just behind us, beyond a long, lonely front. It was deserted apart from a rather harassed-looking young woman walking a dog, and a policeman proceeding slowly along, his blank face as blue with cold as his uniform.

I had been hoping for grandeur, something rather like the Peninsula Hotel in Hong Kong, but our hotel was only a white, four-storey house at the end of a terrace of identical white houses, all a little worn, although they did have rather fancy filigree railings and handsome stone pillars round their doorways. The plaque next to the door read THE LAST RESORT, which made Aunt Lucy and Uncle Felix laugh.

'Won't we have a lovely holiday here?' said Uncle Felix.

'A *holiday*,' said Daisy, raising her eyebrow at him. 'Yes, of course, *won't* we?'

Uncle Felix raised his eyebrow back at her, and

6

for a moment they looked intensely like each other, both so tall and golden and blue.

'Do be a good girl, Daisy,' he told her. '*You* are here to run about on the beach, eating ices. Who Lucy and I happen to meet while we're here . . . well, that is no one's business but our own. Do you understand?'

Daisy rolled her eyes, and the rest of us nodded. I have seen hints of Felix and Lucy's secret life – the coded messages they get at all hours of the night; the times they rushed out of their London flat carrying nothing but their hats, and then stayed away for days before coming back in disguise. It is all quite classified, I know, and I try not to be too curious, but it makes Daisy hungry to discover more.

We went inside, into a foyer with worn leather chairs and a rather chipped chandelier, and windswept guests murmuring politely about the weather. The hotel restaurant and bar were on our right, and the lounge was to our left – I could hear the chink of cups and saucers, the rustle of newspapers, the hum of voices. A chambermaid hurried by, fresh folded towels in her arms, and vanished through a doorway behind the front

desk. A sign at shoulder-height read: THIS WAY
TO ROOMS. GROUND FLOOR: 1–4. FIRST FLOOR: 5–12.
SECOND FLOOR: 13–20. THIRD FLOOR: 21–28.

The desk itself was staffed by a round-faced
man in a smart green and silver-buttoned suit who
introduced himself as the hotel manager, Mr
Geck. He was passing out our keys (Daisy and I
were in Room 3 on the ground floor, while the
boys' room was number 6 on the first floor, where
Aunt Lucy and Uncle Felix, in Room 7, could keep
a respectable, chaperoning eye on them) and
calling for the porter to take our cases, when there
was a commotion in the Last Resort.

All our detective work has taught me to notice
everything, even if it does not seem important, so I
had already been half listening to two women who
were speaking together in low tones in the lounge.
Then I turned as a small, slight woman came
through the front door of the hotel, staggering
under the weight of an enormous, battered suitcase.
I felt rather delighted because I saw that she had
skin as dark as George's. It is always a little gift
not to feel quite so alone among people who look
like Daisy.

At the same moment, a tall, muscular man with

a moustache came through the doorway to the rooms, a towel under his arm. He caught sight of the woman with the suitcase, and then looked beyond her at the women in the lounge – and I saw his handsome face change and redden.

'Now, Toni, we AGREED!' he shouted, and he went storming past us into the lounge.

The two women stopped speaking. One of them – I saw she was holding a notepad and a pen – had an eager look on her face, while the other folded her arms and set her jaw. This woman was pale-skinned, tall and broad-shouldered, and her hair was cut short, just brushing her earlobes. The woman carrying the suitcase went rushing forward in concern, but the tall woman brushed her aside.

'It's all right, Karam. Now, what's up this time, Reggie?' she asked the moustachioed man. The journalist – for I was sure this was what she was – began to write again, scribbling and blinking up at the man in great excitement.

'Oooh, Watson, I recognize that journalist!' Daisy breathed in my ear. She was watching the action too, of course. 'She's quite a famous one – Miss Mottson, from *The Times of London*. And that lady – why, I know who she's talking to! Antonia Braithwaite, the swimmer! She's *the* woman of the moment – she swam the Channel last year, and she's been preparing for the Olympics next week!'

I noticed Mr Geck looking suddenly nervous as he watched the scene, his knuckles white on his desk.

'Didn't we agree, no press?' shouted the man Reggie at Antonia Braithwaite. 'It's hardly fair! You can't spend a day out of the papers!'

'We didn't agree any such thing,' she said coolly. 'I recall you bellowing that at me at the meet in Great Sandmouth earlier this year, but you never gave me a chance to respond. And, if you had, I'd have told you to go away. Why shouldn't I give interviews? The Games are in a few days, and I've a real shot at a medal.'

'Because – because – look here, why don't you want to interview *me*?' said the man, putting his hand rather roughly on Miss Mottson's arm.

'I haven't heard *you* spoken about as a medal hope, Mr Victor,' she said, jerking away from him. 'You haven't won a race in months.'

Reggie Victor turned red. 'See here! I've got

just as much chance as she – and, besides, how am I to win sponsorships if I don't get any press? Toni's taken the Fry's sponsorship, and the Guinness too – how's a fellow to live?'

'Reggie, *do* go away,' said Miss Braithwaite irritably. 'Karam, for heaven's sake, put that case down and show him out, will you? Or get Sam to do it. Sam! I must finish this interview.'

At that, Mr Geck jumped into action. He strode forward, put his hand on Karam's shoulder and whispered in her ear. He was not formal with her as he had been with us, and Karam bent towards him and nodded – they seemed to know each other well. I was fascinated.

'Here, what are you two muttering about?' asked Reggie Victor.

Mr Geck, ignoring him, went hurrying to the front door to wave into the street. Beyond him I saw the policeman, still proceeding slowly along, notice and begin to move rather more quickly towards the Last Resort.

'Sir,' said Mr Geck to Mr Victor, stepping back inside. 'I've just called Constable Neaves over. Now, don't you think it'd be wise for you to leave the ladies alone, before he arrives?'

Mr Victor wilted. He gave Miss Braithwaite, Mr Geck and Karam one more glare, turned on his heel and stormed back the way he had come. Miss Mottson stared after him, making frantic notes on her pad.

'Please do ignore him, Miss Mottson,' said Miss Braithwaite. 'And Sam – call off Neaves, will you?'

'If you're sure, Toni?' said Mr Geck. 'You don't think Reggie will come back and make more trouble?'

'Of course I am!' Miss Braithwaite snapped. 'Oh – I can't stand it. He never leaves me alone!' Her face had gone pale with rage.

'Well, all right,' said Mr Geck, sighing and waving Constable Neaves away.

The women took their seats again, and Mr Geck came back over to us. Everyone tried to behave as though they had not noticed any argument.

'Is that lady ... local?' asked Aunt Lucy, nodding at Antonia Braithwaite.

'She's my half-sister,' said Mr Geck proudly, suddenly smiling. 'Miss Antonia Braithwaite, the Pearl of Saltings! She was born and bred here, like me. She's a very famous swimmer now, but she still remembers where she came from. And Miss Singh is her assistant – we all went to school together, so she's family too, really.' He pulled a wry face. 'Antonia's always been a personality, and Karam was always a timid little mouse – if you ask me, Toni takes advantage of her, but then it seems to work. Now, Evans will show you to your rooms.'

Daisy nudged me as we left the foyer, the porter walking ahead with our suitcases. 'Fascinating, Watson!' she hissed. 'A celebrity swimmer, her jealous rival – and her down-trodden assistant. Could be the makings of an interesting case, don't you think?'

It rained all that afternoon, so heavily that even Daisy could not persuade us to go outside. She fidgeted and grumbled, kneeling up against the tall windows of our room, itching to get out into the wet garden behind the Last Resort. As soon as it began to ease, she wriggled straight out of the window and clattered on to the iron fire escape that snaked up the back of the hotel to pound on the boys' window and declare that she was taking a walk *at once*. I was forced to follow her, even though Daisy knows I don't enjoy heights, a fact which has caused trouble during several of our cases in the past.

'I'll come!' said Alexander, once he had recovered from his shock at seeing us. He opened the window so we could scramble inside.

'We'll all go,' said George. 'And, honestly, you could have come up the ordinary way.'

Daisy scoffed. Daisy Wells never does anything *the ordinary way* if she can help it.

And then we were out of the hotel and walking down to the front, in a landscape that was entirely water. There was water in the sky and under our damp feet, and there to the left of us was a grey sea pressing itself up against a grey beach that stretched out as flat as the palm of a hand and then gathered itself up into lumpy, pebbly hills. It was broken up by long wooden walls that began up by the front and vanished into the sea. They looked rather like ribs, as though the beach had a skeleton. Gulls dived out of the dull sky above us, shrieking, their orange feet and beaks the only bright things I could see. A few families played on the beach, children running screaming in and out of the waves. I clenched my fists inside the pockets of my thin summer mac and tried not to shiver.

'Isn't it lovely?' sighed Daisy, turning her face up to the drizzle. 'Ugh, you're all dreadful. Making me stay cooped up inside when it's like *this*! *I'm* going for a paddle.'

She pulled off her shoes, tucked her socks into them and went scampering away down the beach towards the sea.

'What's a paddle?' I whispered to George – for sometimes I still do not understand English expressions.

'It's when it's too cold to swim, so you just stand in the sea,' George explained.

'Oh!' said Alexander, who is half American, and often as surprised at English things as I am. 'Nothing to do with boats, then?'

'You're all WET!' Daisy shouted up at us. She was in the sea up to her knees, her skirt in a knot.

'CORRECT!' George shouted back, holding out his arms and shaking water droplets off himself. I couldn't help it – I laughed. Alexander did too, and grinned at me, and I felt myself light up.

'Come back, Daisy!' I called. 'I'm freezing.'

'You're BORING!' Daisy shouted – but she came pattering back up the beach, leaving perfect prints in the shingle. 'I've brought my bathing costume, and I mean to swim, whatever you say.'

'We could go swimming tomorrow morning!' said Alexander eagerly.

'Early-morning swimming!' said George. '*Spiffing*, eh?' And he winked at me.

'I'll come if everyone else is,' I said, through gritted teeth.

'Oh, you'll love it!' Daisy said to me blissfully. 'It's the most marvellous feeling.'

I absolutely knew that was a lie.

DAISY

Now it is my turn to write, for this time Hazel shan't have all the fun. Ignore what she has said. *This* account is the true story of the quickest murder mystery the Detective Society has ever solved (and I suppose the boys of our rival agency, the Junior Pinkertons, were also there).

I have looked over the pages that Hazel has already written and I find them lacking, primarily because Hazel, for all that I have taught her well, still does not understand the true joy of the seaside. First of all, it is quite frankly indecent to expect sun when one goes to an English beach. The rain is part of the fun of it. The pebbles should prickle your toes and the water should shock your skin.

You should feel braced, and electrified, and above all *surprised*. Hazel wants the sea to behave like a bathtub because she has *no* sense of adventure.

That was why I wanted us to go for a bathe before breakfast was served on Wednesday, the morning after we arrived in Saltings: to have an adventure. But, I must admit, I was not expecting the kind of adventure we had.

I was first of the four of us outside, of course, because no one else moves fast enough. It was 7:01 by my wristwatch, and the rain had just stopped. Hazel was grumbling about food, just as I knew she would be, but who wants to wait until after breakfast to go for a bathe? Anyway, Uncle Felix and Aunt Lucy had already left on their mission, whatever it was, so *they* weren't bothering with breakfast.

The day had begun misty, and gulls went sweeping above my head, screaming. They were the only things that moved in the stillness apart from me, and I ran and ran, across the road, over the front and onto the beach, as fast as I could to make the world wake up.

I went rattling down the pebbles towards the sand and the sea, wriggling out of my good clothes (my bathing suit was on underneath, of course – a lady never leaves the hotel in just her bathing suit, and we would need to be dressed nicely again for breakfast). The tide was going out, lapping gently away from the silver sand. The others were following behind me (too slow!) and that was why I was the first to see the thing huddled on the shore.

This *thing* was lying on the stones just above the high-tide mark, next to a clump of seaweed stretched out like a hand. I looked at it, all lumpy and discarded in the mist, and I thought to myself immediately: *That's a dead body.* I assumed I was being hopeful and romantic, but I ought to have learned to listen to myself by now. My instincts are always brilliant, and so they were this time.

'What's that?' said George sharply from behind me.

'A seal,' said Alexander. I *cannot* understand how Alexander's mind works. Whoever heard of a seal wearing clothes?

'It's not a seal,' said Hazel. 'Look, oh, look, it's a bathing suit – no, it's *in* a bathing suit.'

'It's a body,' I said, quite certain at this point.

'Quickly!' cried Hazel. 'They might be hurt!'

She and Alexander hared over to it, kneeling

down on the pebbles to shake its shoulders and pat its cheeks.

'It's a woman – the swimmer from yesterday!' gasped Hazel. 'Oh, poor thing – she's so cold!'

I turned to look at George. I hate to admit it, but our minds work in similar ways sometimes, and I saw that this was one of them. His face was set and frowning.

'She's dead, isn't she?' he asked me.

I nodded.

'Daisy!' Hazel called. Her voice wobbled. 'Daisy, she's – she's—'

'And, um,' said Alexander, sitting back on his heels, 'there's something I think you should— George, come here, will you? She – she doesn't smell right.'

'What d'you mean?' I cried, and I went rushing over and knelt down over the body.

Hazel hates describing dead bodies, and that is why I am writing this part. But *I* don't mind saying that when I looked into her face – she had a strong jaw and wide cheekbones – I realized that this was indeed Miss Antonia Braithwaite, the Pearl of Saltings, who had crossed the Channel last year and was one of our hopes for a medal at the Berlin

Olympics the following week. She has been in all the papers. Her bathing costume, I noted, was a Jantzen, suitable for long swims. Her hair was brown, and escaping from under her bathing cap, which had not been put on properly. Her face was not at all nice to look at – but I have seen plenty of dead bodies by now, and I felt reasonably certain from the clues it gave me that she had drowned.

I said this to the others, and they all looked rather horrified.

'Imagine,' said Hazel in a small voice. 'Just yesterday she was alive. We *saw* her. She was full of plans, and – and *life*, and now that's all gone. It's awful!'

I tried not to roll my eyes and remind her that this was exactly how murder worked.

'Yes, but *smell* her, come on!' said Alexander. 'She smells – I can't explain it – all *wrong*!'

I leaned down to the body and sniffed. I hated to admit it, but Alexander was perfectly correct. I ought to have smelled nothing but the sea, salty and sharp, but instead I got a whiff of something else extremely familiar. She smelled clean, soft and fresh – it was the scent of Pears soap.

'She's taken a bath,' I said. 'And she hasn't been

in the sea since, or it would have been washed off.'

'But why would she take a bath and then go to the beach?' asked George.

'Exactly,' said Hazel. 'Why not just stay in the tub where it's warm?'

I glared at her. Hazel is so bold these days, even when faced with dead bodies. 'Antonia Braithwaite is a great athlete,' I said coldly. 'Great athletes do not have time to think about things like *staying warm*. But it is odd.'

I was still kneeling to peer at Miss Braithwaite, and I noticed she had flecks of something on her shoulder, and more on her arm. I thought at first that they were hairs from her head, but they were the wrong colour – a much darker, richer brown – and far too short. I pointed them out to Hazel, and she carefully folded some into her handkerchief.

My heart was beating fast. We had a dead body, a strange smell and some unknown hairs. This felt very much like the beginning of an excellent murder investigation.

And that was when a man came running at us out of the mist.

HAZEL

I gasped, and Daisy shouted, 'STAY BACK!'

The man stumbled backwards, startled. 'I'm just out for a run,' he said. He was pale and broad-chested, with black hair and a rather gorgeous moustache – I realized that we had also seen him yesterday afternoon: Reggie Victor.

'What are you doing here, lurking on the beach like this? And what's wrong with your friend?' He gestured to the body.

'She's not our friend, she's Miss Braithwaite. And she's dead!' I choked out.

Mr Victor stared at the body. His face went absolutely grey.

'What do you mean *dead*?' he cried. 'Nonsense – but— What did you— How—?'

'We found her like this,' said Daisy smoothly, pinching my arm. She was telling me to be on my guard, to watch his reaction. I gave myself a little shake and pulled myself together. 'Do you know her?'

'She – Antonia's a swimmer. Like me. I'm a – and she's rather a – I mean – we – yes, we knew each other,' Mr Victor finished weakly. It was clear that he did not realize we were the people who had overheard their argument yesterday. He was stumbling over his words, gasping, mopping his brow again and again. My detective senses tingled. This man, I thought, was highly suspicious. He knew – and disliked – the victim. He was on the spot. He must be our first suspect.

'But surely we know who you are!' said Daisy, fluttering her eyelashes encouragingly.

Mr Victor took the bait.

'You may well,' he said, drawing himself up. '*I am Reggie Victor.* I won the Templeton Baths Meet this year, and – well – I'm currently in my final week of training for the *Olympic Games.*'

'Oooh!' said Daisy, and only I could hear the mockery in her tone.

'Do you live in Saltings, sir?' asked George.

'I'm staying at a hotel,' said Mr Victor. 'You know, the Last Resort.'

'But that's where we are!' cried Alexander. He sounded so eager and innocent – but then I saw the determined set of his jaw and I knew it was all an act. The Pinkertons were as focused on detection as Daisy and I were. 'See here, shouldn't someone go and get the police?'

'You all ought to go,' said Mr Victor, trying to look heroic. I found this even more suspicious than his manner before. 'I'll stay here. You're kids – you don't need to see this.'

'Oh, sir, we can't just leave you!' said George. 'I'll stay too. Alex, you take the girls.'

I saw the angry spark in Daisy's eye, and I knew that leaving the body – and with the Junior Pinkertons, who, as much as they were our friends, would always be our detecting rivals in Daisy's mind – was the last thing she wanted to do. Now that George had suggested it, she had to play along, but she would do it on her own terms.

'Oh no, Alex must stay as well!' she said. 'We'll be quite all right on our own, won't we, Hazel?

This is really *too* horrid – we're better off waiting in the hotel while you brave boys stay here to guard the body until that *excellent* policeman arrives.'

She and George stared at each other for a moment, and then George nodded and said, 'All right, Daisy.'

Only I could see the tremble of her lips as she tried not to laugh. I realized what she had done. She had freed us up to investigate clues at the hotel, while the Junior Pinkertons were stuck with a body we had already looked at.

We stepped away up the beach together, Daisy quickly pulling on her clothes again, leaving George, Alexander and Mr Victor standing over Miss Braithwaite's huddled body. The mist was still thick, and Daisy had to catch my arm several times as I stumbled over the stones.

'Do you think they'll be all right with him?' I whispered to her as soon as we had moved out of earshot. 'What if he – what if he *did it*?'

'He's not likely to hurt them either way,' Daisy said, shrugging. 'He has no idea we're anything more than a group of silly schoolchildren. But, Hazel, that's not important. What *is* important is that, before that clodhopper Neaves arrives to ruin everything, we must get into the dead woman's room, and Mr Victor's, and find out all we can about them both!'

DAISY

I thought we should never get away from the Junior Pinkertons to begin our investigation in earnest. Hazel is so obsessed with that boy Alexander – although he is not *half* as clever as she is, and his arms are *too long*, still she pines after him. Dull.

But at last we escaped, and I was free to run and run and run all the way back to the hotel – but I did not lead Hazel through the front door once she had caught up. That would have been a terrible error. No, I paused and told her about my excellent plan.

'We must go to the front desk together,' I said. 'I shall inform whoever's there in my prettiest voice that there is a dead body on the beach. They will panic and, while they're busy running about and fetching that bumbling Neaves man, we can scan the visitors' book for Miss Braithwaite's and Mr Victor's names at our leisure. Then we shall have the time it takes *him* to arrive and mess about with interviews – I estimate at least twenty minutes – to detect unhindered. The chambermaids won't go in to tidy the rooms until everyone is at breakfast, after all, and it's still only twenty-five past seven.'

'But how are we going to get into the rooms?' asked Hazel. 'Oh, wait, I know! We can get out of our bedroom window like we did yesterday, go up the fire escape and see if any of the other windows are open.'

I felt . . . well, not resentful, for Hazel is my best friend and I am perfectly aware by this point that she sometimes has ideas almost as excellent as mine. But certainly I was . . . taken aback somewhat. It had been exactly what I was about to say, but I had not quite got round to saying it yet.

'I *was* going to say that there are other ways to get into a room,' I said at last. 'We may not need to use the fire escape.'

'You were *not* going to say that,' said Hazel. 'You just invented it because I said your idea.'

'Silence, Watson,' I said, sticking out my tongue at her crossly. 'It's true. I've heard of an excellent way to get into a hotel room using only a teaspoon. Now, before we begin, do we have any more facts that could be of use? Did either of us hear anything or see anything that might be relevant?'

'Apart from that argument yesterday?' asked Hazel. 'I've been trying to think, but nothing particularly – we went to bed at ten last night, we woke up at a quarter to seven, and we went out for a bathe. *Before* breakfast!'

'Hmm,' I said. 'Yes, but there is one thing. I remember half waking up in the night and hearing a bath running.'

Hazel gazed at me. 'You don't think – no!' she said, sickened. 'You don't think you heard the murder?'

'I don't know,' I said slowly. 'But it may be important. It was at eleven p.m. by my wristwatch. Bear it in mind as you search the room – not all of them have bathrooms, so we may be able to work out which one it was. Now, are you ready? As soon as we've announced Miss Braithwaite's death, we shall only have a few minutes in which to work.'

Hazel set her chin and nodded.

'All right. Let us begin the case in earnest!'

HAZEL

This sort of detective work always leaves me feeling unsettled.

Mr Geck, as smartly dressed as yesterday and sorting through the morning papers at the front desk, seemed appalled when we told him what we had discovered on the beach. His rather round, friendly face turned absolutely white, and he could only stammer in shock. He looked about frantically, gasping and absolutely forgetting to order anyone to take his place or to telephone the police station. That bought us more time, of course, but I could not feel glad about it, for we had just informed him that his sister had died.

We watched him stumble out of the front door towards the beach. I was thinking about my own

31

little sisters. Daisy gave me a sharp poke in the ribs. 'Buck up, Watson! He's a suspect too, since he was the victim's half-brother. Come on – we must act quickly.'

We waited as an old guest in a lacy wrap picked up a newspaper and shuffled into the lounge, and then we were free to slip behind the front desk to look at the visitors' book.

Antonia Braithwaite was in Room 1, and Reggie Victor in Room 4, both on the ground floor, just as we were. That was an odd thought – that the players in this mystery had been so close to us, *and* to each other.

'Yes, indeed,' said Daisy, catching my thoughts. 'Interesting, isn't it? Well, I know at least one thing: this will make it terrifically easy for us to detect. We don't even need to climb the fire escape again! Isn't that useful for you, Hazel?'

I glared at her.

'I shall take Miss Braithwaite's room, of course,' said Daisy, who always gives herself the plum jobs, 'and you can look at Mr Victor's. Agreed?'

'Agreed,' I said with a sigh.

'Excellent,' said Daisy. 'And now, Hazel, I shall have to put my teaspoon plan into practice. How useful that breakfast has already been laid out. I trust I do not need to explain to you how to search a room?'

Daisy, for all we have solved eight murder mysteries together, still has very little faith in anyone who is not herself.

Daisy and I crouched together at Reggie Victor's door. Daisy had unscrewed its handle, and she was wriggling a breakfast teaspoon around in the hole where it ought to sit. She gave it one last determined prod, and then, just as I was convinced we would have to give up, the door creaked open.

'There!' said Daisy. 'See?'

I stood up, sighing, and stepped inside, while she went on to Room 1.

I got a surprise when I saw the room, for I had expected it to be the image of ours – all pale blue chintz and potted plants and fringed lamps. But this room was rather more masculine, red papered walls covered with sporting scenes and a large iron-framed bed, its sheets tumbled back restlessly. The air smelled of cologne, and there was a ewer and basin with shaving things next to the bed – this was not one of the rooms with a bath.

I felt rather intimidated.

But nevertheless I went to work – and, as I did so, my suspicions about Mr Victor hardened. I was very glad he had decided to go for a run on the beach. He had left all his things behind, not bothering to lock them away in the hotel safe: his passport, a hopelessly unbalanced chequebook (he was several hundred pounds in debt, which made me feel rather queasy), and a pile of letters from sponsors withdrawing their support following poor performances (so there was no money coming in, either). On the side there were pots of pills and potions and muscle creams that promised renewed vigour. The story was clear: Reggie Victor was no longer a swimmer at the top of his game and, since he was not winning races or being sponsored any more, he was facing money troubles. Now I understood why he had been so cross with Miss Braithwaite yesterday. But could this be a motive for him to have committed murder?

I had found out what I could from this room – now I wanted to see what clues Daisy had uncovered.

DAISY

The victim's door opened easily. I was proud of my new skills as a locksmith. I slipped inside and looked around.

The window was a touch open. *So we could have come in through the garden!* I thought. The room – with a bathroom attached, I noticed – was well ordered. I saw at once what sort of person Miss Braithwaite had been: one who was absolutely dedicated to her sport. There were pictures of her dotted about the room: Antonia swimming; Antonia with medals round her neck. There were weights for her to exercise with, and training schedules. I had a look at one, and saw dates neatly ticked off. This was a woman whose whole life had been preparing for her next competition.

I was rather impressed. It is usually Hazel who feels sad for the victims (and even the murderers. Hazel's heart is much too soft and kind, no matter how I try to teach her), but I felt . . . sorry, I must admit, that this woman would never get to the Olympics. It is always nice to see someone be the best at something, as I am the best at detecting, and she was the very best swimmer England had to offer. She had crossed the Channel faster than any man has ever managed – but now she would not be around to show the world how excellent she was.

I shook myself out of this daydream and got to work. What else could I glean about Miss Braithwaite?

There was a sheet of paper on the writing desk, much scribbled over and crossed out. At the top it said *Last Will and Testament of Antonia Braithwaite* – it was not signed, and looked very much unfinished, but I scanned it quickly. All her money – quite a considerable amount – was to be left to Karam Singh and Samuel Geck, divided between them equally. This was interesting: was it a motive for Miss Singh and Mr Geck, or did it rule them out, because the will was not yet signed? And why had such a careful woman not left this in the hotel safe?

The bed was neatly made, and her clothes folded in their drawers – there, again, was the tidy person who had created all those schedules. Antonia Braithwaite did not seem much interested in fashion, or beauty. There were only two simple rings and a few necklaces in her jewellery box, and only a powder compact and a lipstick on her chest of drawers. Next to that, though, I saw something much more interesting: a tray with a bottle and two glasses, both empty. I sniffed at them and, although they seemed to have been rather badly rinsed, I smelled alcohol. But in one glass there was something else as well – something that made me stand up straighter in surprise. It was a sleeping draught, I was sure of it.

Then I ducked my head into the bathroom, and found quite a different scene. It was not tidy at all – water had been splashed about as though a whale had been bathing there. A towel had been put down to mop it up, but water was all over the floor, where a heap of damp clothes was soaking in it. A half-melted cake of Pears soap still lurked where it had slipped to the bottom of the tub, along with a slick of soapy water.

A lesser mind than mine might have struggled to make sense of the scene, but, what with this and the glasses, I was beginning to piece things together – and an unpleasant picture they made too.

I suddenly had a thought, and went darting out of the bathroom to the wardrobe. I pulled it open, and there – I had hardly dared hope, but – there was a woman's thick, luscious fur coat, in a rich brown colour. I needed to check it against the hairs Hazel had in her handkerchief, but I was convinced they would match.

I reached out and ran my fingers lightly over the fur. *And it was damp.* Damp inside and out, with a smell on the lining (I leaned forward and sniffed carefully) of clean soap and water. And, at the place where the sleeve met the body, a small tear in the lining that looked new.

I felt electrified. A damp, torn coat. Water still in the bath, and a heap of wet clothes beside it. A bottle and two glasses, one smelling of something to put you to sleep. A body lying on the beach with the scent of soap.

I heard footsteps behind me and I whirled about in triumph.

'*I know what happened to Antonia Braithwaite!*' I said.

HAZEL

I pushed open the unlocked door and stepped into Antonia Braithwaite's room to find Daisy poised in the middle of the floor, eyes blazing and arms outstretched. She did not seem at all surprised to see me.

'Hazel, you absolutely must listen to me!' she cried. 'I know exactly what happened! Of course, I don't know the murderer's name yet, but that will come. Hazel, *I know everything*.'

'*Except* the murderer's name,' I repeated, making a face at her.

'Quiet!' hissed Daisy. '*Don't* speak. *Listen*. Now, we both inspected the body, didn't we? So we can verify that it smelled of soap, not the sea. Yes?'

'Yes,' I said.

Daisy glared at me.

'I told you, *do not speak*! Now, I have looked at the victim's room, and what have I found? There is a bathroom, and it's in *terrible* disarray. There's water all over the floor, clothes in a wet heap and soap still at the bottom of the tub. And what, added to the fact that I heard a bath running last night, does that tell you?'

I caught my breath. 'You think she drowned – in *this* bath! She was murdered *here* last night and then carried to the beach!'

Daisy narrowed her eyes. She always hates it when other people steal her denouements. 'Indeed,' she said at last. 'But that is only the beginning of my deduction. There are two glasses and one of them smells odd – I think Miss Braithwaite was drugged before she was murdered! I have been wondering why I didn't hear anything apart from the bath last night, seeing as we were so close, and that would explain it. She wasn't awake to struggle!

'Then I looked in the wardrobe and I found a brown fur coat, with fur that I believe matches the hairs we discovered – a damp coat that *also* smells of soap. And I understood how the body was moved. After she was drowned, she was undressed and then put into her swimming things – remember that ill-fitting bathing cap? Then she was wrapped in her fur coat, and carried to the beach. It was raining last night, remember, so no one else was likely to have been out – and of course that's why the coat is still damp, and a little torn.'

'But why the coat at all?' I asked, pulling out my handkerchief and giving it to Daisy, who made a pleased noise when she saw the hairs. 'Oh! You think – to make things look ordinary, in case someone *did* see them?'

'Exactly,' said Daisy, twinkling at me. 'A lady in a fur coat being helped along by a friend after a long night out is quite uninteresting. And this, along with the running bath I heard, gives us a strong idea of *when* the murder and the moving of the body took place – some time after eleven last night and before the rain stopped this morning. Then the coat was returned to the wardrobe.'

I frowned. 'But, if there was time to bring the coat back, why not clean up the scene of the crime too, instead of leaving such a mess? And why take her all the way to the beach? Was she supposed to have been swept out to sea and not found?'

'No,' said Daisy, and I saw the crease at the top of her nose deepen as she thought about it. 'No, she was left above the high-tide mark – which means the water would never come up to cover her. I noticed that at once. She couldn't have been swept away unless there was a storm – and no storm's been forecast. What if—'

But there she was brought up short, because suddenly the door to Antonia Braithwaite's room opened and Karam Singh, the small dark woman we had seen with Antonia yesterday, stepped inside.

We froze, and I heard myself gasp.

'What on earth are you doing here?' demanded Miss Singh.

DAISY

I thought on my feet, which is something all the best detectives must be able to do.

'Ah, Miss Singh!' I said. 'Thank goodness you're here. Mr Geck's been looking for you.'

'Sam?' asked Miss Singh. 'Why?' She was frowning, distracted, and she looked around the room as though she hardly cared that we were there.

'It's because of Miss Braithwaite,' I said, and her eyes came back to mine, and went wide and frightened.

'What happened?' she asked. Now, I have been a detective for several years, and I thought that an odd question. I had not said anything other than Miss Braithwaite's name, but here was her friend, assuming the worst.

'Oh *dear*,' said Hazel, and I nudged her as hard as I could to tell her not to be wet and sorry for a suspect – for since Miss Singh was named in Antonia Braithwaite's will, I had decided that we must add her to the suspect list, along with Mr Geck, until we could detect further.

'Her bed hasn't been slept in,' said Miss Singh, pointing as she moved across the room. 'And what on earth's happened in the bathroom?'

'You – you might want to sit down. I'm afraid we have some news,' said Hazel gently. 'Miss Braithwaite— There's been an accident. I'm terribly sorry. She's – she's dead.'

Miss Singh froze.

'Nonsense,' she snapped, and her eyes snapped too, sharp and black. I suddenly saw the shadow of someone else beneath the sweet politeness, someone firm and fierce. 'Of course she's not *dead*. She's going to the Olympics next week. She can't be *dead*. Who told you she was?'

'We saw her,' said Hazel apologetically. 'We found the body.'

'Nonsense!' cried Miss Singh again, glancing at

her wristwatch. 'It's five to eight – she's out for her morning swim. She'll be back at eight for breakfast, and then you'll see!'

Hazel and I exchanged a look, and I felt delighted that the same understanding still flowed between us.

'You know rather a lot about her schedule,' I said.

'Of course I do,' said Miss Singh wildly. 'Who do you think drew it up? Who do you think planned it all? Who d'you think manages the sponsorships and the journalists and the training? Why, Antonia hasn't an organized bone in her body – never has, and I've known her since we were ten years old. If I didn't lay out her life for her, she'd miss everything. I'm even drawing up her will for her – she's looking through it at the moment. She went travelling without me once and it was a disaster. *Not* that she thanks me for it, most of the time.'

I am not ordinarily cross with myself, but I was briefly cross now. It had not occurred to me that Antonia might be tidy because someone else was tidying for her – and it ought to have done. First impressions, after all, can be misleading, and a good detective should never simply accept the obvious answer.

'You must know her very well,' said Hazel, still gentle.

'She's my best friend,' said Miss Singh. 'And she can't be dead. It's nonsense, I tell you.'

'Of course it's not nonsense!' I cried. I was tired of this. 'It's absolutely true. Miss Braithwaite is dead, and you stood to profit from her death. The question is, where were *you* at eleven o'clock last night?'

HAZEL

Sometimes I wish Daisy were not quite so ... Daisyish. She simply leaps to conclusions and forgets how other people work. I saw the horror on Miss Singh's face, and I knew that Daisy had made a mistake.

'It's none of your business!' she gasped. 'I don't even know who you are! Get out of Toni's room! Get OUT! SAM! SAM! HELP!'

And, of course, we had to leave.

'*Daisy!*' I hissed as the door slammed behind us.

Daisy glared at me. 'What ought I to have said?' she asked. 'She was being idiotic. Grown-ups never listen! She needed to understand.'

'But – her friend died,' I said. 'You heard: best

friends since they were ten, Daisy. They're just like us!'

'They are *not* like us,' grumbled Daisy. 'First of all, we didn't meet until we were eleven. And, second, neither of us will ever die. I won't allow it, Hazel.'

'*Exactly!*' I said, sharper than I meant to. 'That's it. If someone told you I'd died, you'd never believe it.'

'Do be quiet, Hazel. That is not relevant. What *is* relevant is the other information we heard in the course of our interrogation.'

'I'm not sure that was an—' I began.

'*What did we hear?*' Daisy pushed on, through gritted teeth.

'Miss Singh said Miss Braithwaite hadn't been to bed,' I said, sighing. 'She might be lying, of course, but the bed didn't look slept in – and that fits with the timing of the bath you heard. Miss Braithwaite was making a will, which would have left all her money to Miss Singh and to her brother, Sam – Mr Geck. And Miss Singh organizes everything for her, even her sponsorships. What if she thinks that Miss Braithwaite's been taking her for granted, and she wanted some of that money?'

'But there's a problem with that,' said Daisy. 'The will isn't signed – Miss Braithwaite never got the chance to. So that motive doesn't quite work. Unless – what if Miss Singh wasn't happy with just half? What if she's been squirrelling away Miss Brathwaite's money, and didn't like the idea of it being divided up between her and Mr Geck? She could have decided to take matters into her own hands.'

'Well, all right, say she did,' I said. 'Say she knocked out Miss Braithwaite with a sleeping draught – how could she have even lifted her into the bath, let alone carried her all the way to the beach? Miss Braithwaite was tall and strong, and Miss Singh's smaller than I am.'

'Easy!' said Daisy. 'I'm sure she could. I'll show you. Hazel, hold me.'

She suddenly slumped, making me catch her. I got a thumping blow from her shoulder, yelped and staggered forward. Daisy was a dead weight, astonishingly heavy, and I was shocked.

'Ow! Daisy!' I gasped. 'Stop it! Please! I can't do it!'

'Yes you can, Hazel!' said Daisy. 'Go on, go at it properly!'

Then I heard a voice say, 'Whatever are you two doing?'

DAISY

It was George, his arms crossed. It must have begun to rain again, for his hair was slicked down with water. He looked amused. Alexander was standing just behind him.

'We are carrying out a reconstruction,' I told him with dignity. 'What are you two doing? Why aren't you still with the body? This is dreadful detective work. We gave you one job!'

'A job you didn't want!' said George. 'And Mr Victor didn't try to kill us, thank you for asking. He only ranted on about Miss Braithwaite dying. I think he's almost upset that his competition's gone – or perhaps that's just an act. Anyway, we had to leave when that Neaves man, the neighbourhood bobby, arrived. I think he's the only policeman in Saltings – and Mr Geck said he's new here, so he's hopeless. Doesn't have the first idea of what to do. He touched the body and rolled it about when he was searching it for clues! We tried to stop him, only it was no good, and we were beginning to look suspicious. We left Mr Victor arguing with him and came to find you – only we got caught by Mr Geck. He's in a terrible state – he's so upset he's *telling* us things.'

Inside I raged. I am so tired of useless, clod-hopping policemen ruining our cases! But there was nothing to be done – we simply had to reveal the real murderer, and quickly, before this Neaves person arrived at the wrong answer.

'You have to come and talk to him,' said Alexander. 'The stuff he told us sounds important.'

We all hurried out to the foyer, where we found Mr Geck slumped against the desk, his head buried in his hands. He pulled himself upright when he heard us coming.

'Oh dear!' cried Hazel. 'I'm sorry!'

I did not say anything, for I never can see the point of polite nothings. And anyway I was suspicious. How could we be sure that this grief was not simply a clever ruse to throw us off the scent?

Mr Geck gave a sob.

'*I'm* sorry – this is terribly unprofessional of me – but Toni's *gone!*' he choked out.

'But you saw something, didn't you, sir?' said Alexander encouragingly. 'You were telling us – something happened last night. In the bar.'

'Mr Geck,' George explained, 'also works at the Last Resort's bar.'

'Everyone's more than one thing here,' muttered Mr Geck. 'The postman's our chef some evenings. Antonia used to be one of the chambermaids, when I was the porter. But now she's our Pearl – I mean, she *was*.' His face twisted with sorrow. 'She travels all over – we didn't see her for a year while she was in foreign parts – but, when she's back in Saltings, she always stays here. That way we can see one another, and Karam – Miss Singh – and I can make sure reporters don't get to her without an appointment. We were *protecting* her, and now—'

He gave another sob, and Hazel and Alexander made encouraging noises. I was simply desperate to get to the story. And I could see that George was too.

'So, the bar,' he said carefully. 'Everyone was there, weren't they?'

I felt frustrated. If only *we* had been there too, instead of asleep – but, once again, we were foiled by our ages! Oh, how I long to rush forward in time and simply *become* twenty.

'Yes, Toni and Karam were at the bar with the journalist – Miss Mottson, I think – and so was that fellow Reggie Victor. He's washed up, and that's a fact. I can always tell the desperate ones. There's a certain look in their eyes, and he had it. He snarled at Toni and Karam – Toni looked flustered; she was odd all evening, kept checking her watch – and then began to flirt with Miss Mottson. I think it was really to annoy Toni, though Miss Mottson took the bait wonderfully. They left together at about half past ten, and then Toni looked at her watch again and said, "I think we should call it a night." Karam turned to go, and Toni leaned over the bar at me and whispered, "Sam, can you send a bottle of whiskey and two glasses to my room in fifteen minutes?"

'I was curious – I asked her why, but Antonia wouldn't say, just shook her head. So I knocked on her door at a quarter to eleven, and she opened it, just a crack, and took the tray from me. I couldn't see inside – she was careful about that – but I heard a voice, and I think . . . well, I think there was *a man* in her room.'

I was intrigued. I felt my hands clench, my breath short in my chest.

'Did you know the voice?' I asked.

Mr Geck shook his head, a frown on his face. 'I don't *know*,' he said, frustrated. 'I thought he sounded familiar, but I can't be sure.'

'Hmm,' I said. 'Now, det— er, Hazel, Alexander and George, I think we need to go and have a . . . chat. Come along quickly!'

'Thank you!' Hazel called over her shoulder as I hurried the three of them away.

It was time for a Detective Society meeting.

HAZEL

Of course, this was the perfect opportunity to have breakfast, and a bunbreak. Bunbreak is an important part of our detective work. It's really the word for the biscuits we eat every morning at school, but nothing helps detection like sweet food, and so we make sure to have several bunbreaks during each of our cases, even the ones in the holidays.

We went hurrying across the foyer to the dining room and sat down at our places. The waitress (a chambermaid with an apron on over her uniform) looked at us rather askance when Daisy asked for iced buns along with the usual bacon and eggs – for it was only just after eight in the morning – but, under the circumstances, buns for breakfast felt like the only thing that would do. As we ordered, I saw Aunt Lucy and Uncle Felix walking by on the front, talking to a man wearing dark glasses, but I carefully ignored them.

The Case of the Body at the Seaside, I wrote down, as we all bent over my casebook. *Present: Daisy Wells, Hazel Wong, George Mukherjee and Alexander Arcady.*

We waited until our breakfasts (and extra buns) were in front of us, and then we took a deep breath and began.

'All right. What do we know?' asked Daisy.

'A woman's dead,' said George.

'Very imprecise,' said Daisy scornfully. 'The Olympic hopeful Antonia Braithwaite is dead – found drowned on Saltings beach this morning just after seven a.m. The suspects are—'

'Aren't the *clues* the important thing in this case?' asked George. 'She was found smelling of soap, not seawater. She had hairs on her bathing suit, and when you went to her room you found a fur coat that matched those hairs.'

'You're taking things out of order!' Daisy snapped. '*Suspects* first!'

George and Daisy glared at each other. They both enjoy being in charge, and do not really know what to do when challenged. Alexander and I shared a sympathetic look, and then I turned towards Daisy and said, 'All right. The suspects are Reggie Victor, Miss Braithwaite's sporting competitor, Sam Geck, her brother, and Karam Singh, Miss Braithwaite's assistant.'

'And now motives for each of them, if you please, Watson.'

I ticked them off on my fingers. 'We know Mr Victor resented Miss Braithwaite's success, and he's struggling for money at the moment. Perhaps Mr Geck was cross at being left behind, working in the family hotel, while his sister travelled the world? And Miss Singh is Miss Braithwaite's friend from school, the one who organized her life, and she might have resented Miss Braithwaite taking advantage as Mr Geck mentioned.' I frowned. 'Then there's the will. If it had been signed, then that would be an extra motive for both Mr Geck and Miss Singh – but it wasn't finished . . .' I tailed off. I wasn't quite sure what the will told us.

'Can we move on to the facts in the case *now*?' asked George.

Daisy glared at him.

'The body was on the beach, above the high-water mark. She was only wearing a bathing costume and cap – but at some point she had also been dressed in a fur coat, a coat that is back in her wardrobe this morning,' I said. 'This, and what Mr Geck says he heard, tell us that the murderer had access to her room. They were there a quarter to eleven, and Daisy heard the bath running at eleven – so the murder must have happened after that time. Daisy, you think that the murderer drugged Miss Braithwaite's drink, took her into the bathroom and drowned her in the bath.'

'I don't *think*,' said Daisy, 'I use the facts to lead me to a conclusion. It's quite different. It is also interesting that the real crime scene was not tidied away, and the murderer allowed the soap to slip into the bath and perfume the corpse – the whole crime seems so badly planned!'

'Mr Geck's story is interesting, isn't it?' asked George. 'The man's voice?'

'He might be lying,' said Daisy. 'He might have made up the whole story to seem more innocent. What if he was the person who brought the glasses to her room with one already drugged, and then killed her?'

'He might,' said George, nodding. 'That's very true. That's one possibility. If he *is* lying, he's the murderer. But if he's telling the truth—'

'Hey!' said Alexander. 'I get it! If he's telling the truth, then the murderer's a man – so it can't be Miss Singh, right?'

I suddenly remembered the dead weight of Daisy slumped against me. 'From that reconstruction Daisy and I did, we know that Miss Singh couldn't have carried Miss Braithwaite's body to the beach, either!' I put in, looking at Daisy.

She frowned. 'Hazel, you are simply weak. I don't think you were trying hard enough.'

'I *was*!' I said indignantly. 'It couldn't be done. She's too small, her voice doesn't sound deep enough – and she's too tidy, as well! This isn't the crime of a tidy person, don't you see?'

Daisy sighed. 'Oh, all right,' she said reluctantly.

'We definitely have to rule her out. That leaves us with Mr Victor and Mr Geck. But, if the murderer was Mr Victor, why would Miss Braithwaite have made an appointment to meet him in her room? She didn't like him.'

'That *is* odd,' agreed George. 'And there's something else. Why did he – or Mr Geck – take her all the way to the beach? We keep asking this, and it's important. Of course, it would have been easy to do in the rain last night – but still, why? Was it supposed to look like an accident? Her being above the high-water mark – which means the sea couldn't have washed her away – was that on purpose? Was she *supposed* to have been found so soon?'

'Here's another question we keep running up against: why murder her before the will was finished?' asked Alexander. 'If it was her brother, he's more likely to benefit if she finished and signed it, right? So maybe that points to Mr Victor.'

'Whichever of them it is, he's done a dreadful job of covering up his tracks,' said Daisy. 'The crime was so poorly cleaned up, which is odd, since the murderer had all the hours between eleven, when I heard the bath running, and seven ten, when we found the body. It speaks to a *very* slow and lazy mind.'

'See here,' said Alexander, his face brightening. 'I've just had a thought. I can imagine a very good reason for Mr Victor to need to murder her before her will was finished, *and* a reason why she might let him into her room too.'

'Go on, Alex,' said George.

'Well, who's next of kin who isn't family?' he asked. 'Someone you're *married* to. What if – what if Mr Victor and Miss Braithwaite were secretly *married*, and only pretending to hate each other? That could explain why she let him in, why they're staying at the same hotel, and why the body *had* to be found looking as though she'd drowned. So she'd be registered as dead by misadventure, and all the money would go as quickly as possible . . . to her husband.'

'Good heavens,' said Daisy, rather faintly. 'That is . . . why, that is either arrant nonsense or rather intelligent detective work. And I did find those rings in her jewellery box . . . it would make sense. How annoying. Hazel, write all this down immediately! We have several questions we need to answer at once!'

SUSPECT LIST

1. *Reggie Victor* — seen arguing with the victim the day before her death. An angry, violent person who is in desperate need of money. What if he is secretly married to Antonia Braithwaite, meaning he benefits from her death?

2. ~~Karam Singh~~ — the victim's
~~assistant and old schoolfriend. She~~
~~manages everything for her —~~
~~including the making of her will!~~
RULED OUT. She is simply too
small to carry Miss Braithwaite
from her room to the beach, and Mr
Geck's witness statement — whether
or not it is true — also shows she
can't be involved.

3. Sam Geck — the victim's brother,
and the hotel manager. What if he
resents his sister for her success, and
wants to kill her for her money? He
says he saw the victim alive at 10:45
p.m., when he brought glasses and a
bottle of whiskey to her room, just
before Daisy heard the bath running.
If he is lying, he is the murderer.
If he is telling the truth, Reggie
Victor is the murderer!

DAISY

We jumped up from our seats at breakfast (several hotel guests tutted) and hurried back out into the foyer. I felt convinced that something was happening without me, and so it was. Mr Geck had now pulled himself together to look halfway presentable. He nodded at us.

'Constable Neaves is here,' he said dully. 'I told him everything I told you. He'll sort this out.'

I was horrified.

'Quick!' I cried. 'We must follow him before he ruins the case!'

I was not entirely sure, in the moment, what I thought might happen, but I was determined to stop it anyway. I hared past the front desk towards the rooms, Hazel, Alexander and George following. Antonia Braithwaite's door was open, and we rushed inside . . . to find Constable Neaves standing next to her chest of drawers.

The constable was a most unattractive man, I thought at that moment – all bug-eyed and pale-faced. But, more importantly, he was reaching out for the two glasses – and he was NOT wearing gloves.

I was scandalized. What a clodhopper! Why, he was about to contaminate the crime scene! It was clear that he was in no fit state to lead this investigation.

'Stop immediately!' I cried.

'Daisy!' said Hazel. I ignored her. This was no time to be Hazel-ish and cautious.

'Stop, I say! This is an important investigation, and you're ruining it,' I snapped.

Our raised voices had been heard. Mr Geck appeared in the doorway, Reggie Victor, Miss Mottson and Karam Singh just behind him.

'See here!' said Reggie. 'You children shouldn't interfere with police business!'

'What do you mean?' Constable Neaves asked me slowly, ignoring Mr Geck. At that moment, I could have slapped him. 'Miss Braithwaite drowned. I'm merely looking through her room to confirm that it was an accident and not – well . . . you know.'

'It wasn't an accident at all! Someone drowned her!' said Alexander. Mr Geck made a noise. Constable Neaves's frown deepened.

'Have you lot been playing detective?' he asked, eyeing the four of us. 'Telling yourself stories? The poor woman drowned in the sea. It's quite clear to me.'

I clutched at Hazel's arm, gasping. It could not be! I had been prepared for him to get the wrong murderer, but not for him to assume that there was no murderer at all!

'See here, are you sure?' asked Mr Victor from the doorway, as Miss Mottson craned round him eagerly, notebook in hand. 'I know Antonia was infuriating, but I don't think – I don't think that fits. She was a good swimmer, and she knew the sea here. I don't think it was an accident.'

'Of course it wasn't!' said Mr Geck. 'Neaves, you can't be serious. My sister wouldn't drown, not at *our* beach. She's been swimming there since she was a baby! I told you I heard a man in her room, at a quarter to eleven – I've been thinking, and I'm sure now that it was Mr Victor.'

Reggie Victor jumped. 'What? NONSENSE!' he roared at Mr Geck, who looked offended.

My head was spinning, and when I looked at Hazel she seemed as puzzled as I felt. Why should both our remaining suspects insist that Antonia Braithwaite's death was murder, when we had just concluded that leaving the body on the beach was designed to make it look like an accident?

Suddenly I knew what I needed to ask.

'Why was Miss Braithwaite making a will?' I said to Miss Singh. 'Why *now*? Quickly! And *don't* say that you won't tell me because I'm too young.'

She looked puzzled and hesitant – oh, people are so frustrating! They are always three steps behind me, and it makes me itch with annoyance. 'It's important!' I said. 'If – if you tell me, I think I can tell you who killed Miss Braithwaite.'

'But— Oh, I don't see that it matters any more!' said Miss Singh, and I saw that there were tears in her eyes. Silly! 'It was because of the Olympics – the money she might win, you know. It was more money than either of us had ever – well – if she got a medal, Toni would be really quite rich suddenly.

And that worried her. She kept saying she needed to make a will now because it was the only way to— Oh – well, I shouldn't say.'

'Now really, you must!' said Miss Mottson, who seemed as fascinated as we were. 'My readers will want to know!'

'Well, she didn't want *a certain person* to get any,' said Miss Singh reluctantly. 'When she went away for that year, when she travelled, she *met someone*. Those rings she always keeps in her jewellery box – they're engagement and wedding rings. She didn't want to talk about it, or tell me who he is, but . . . that's why we travel about so much. She regretted the marriage, you see. He's been following her, and sending her letters, pleading with her to come back to him.'

A husband! So we were right! Miss Mottson looked quite electrified.

'You!' cried Mr Geck. He was pointing at Mr Victor. 'You – you – *you're* the husband, aren't you? That's why you followed her here! To kill her, before she could make her will!'

'Of course I'm not the HUSBAND!' shouted Mr Victor. 'I've never been married in my LIFE. That's NOT my style. If you want to know what

I was doing last night, well – Miss Mottson, tell them!'

'Ah,' said Miss Mottson, and her cheeks suddenly turned pink. 'Well – I happened to have been in Mr Victor's company all evening, after we left the bar. Simply interviewing him, you know,' she added quickly. 'I certainly don't think he could have had the opportunity to be the man Mr Geck heard.'

So Mr Geck was lying, after all! But then – what about the husband?

'I – I think you ought all to calm down,' said Neaves. 'This is NOT a murder investigation. I've told you. Toni simply drowned!'

And I suddenly had a brainwave. I knew – everything. I knew who had killed Antonia Braithwaite, and why. I knew why the body had been posed so that it looked like an accident, and why the crime scene had not been tidied away. I knew why Miss Braithwaite had let her killer into her room and had a drink with him.

'Mr Victor didn't kill anyone,' I said. 'Neither did Miss Singh, or Mr Geck.'

'But then – who did?' asked Alexander.

I looked at Hazel, and she looked back at me.

And, once again, understanding flowed perfectly between us.

'The person who just gave himself away by calling Antonia Braithwaite by her nickname,' she said. 'The man who arrived at the scene of the crime without ever having been called, and who has just been trying to tidy it away. Her husband. *Constable Neaves.*'

I saw the colour entirely drain from Neaves's face, and I knew that we were right.

HAZEL

I felt the exact moment when the case clicked into place, like a door slamming shut. The window to the garden in Antonia Braithwaite's room had been open – of course, she could have let someone from Saltings in on the night of her murder. She might have arranged a meeting with her husband without telling her friend Miss Singh – some things, after all, even best friends do not talk about.

Constable Neaves was the man whose voice Mr Geck had heard. He was strong enough to carry Miss Braithwaite's body to the beach – and his uniform would have given him a perfect excuse, if anyone saw him helping a lady along late at night. He left her above the high-water mark so the sea couldn't sweep her away, and she would be discovered quickly – and, although he had quickly rinsed out the glasses, mopped at the water in the bathroom and put back the coat, he had not bothered to do anything more because he had planned to arrive on the scene before anyone went into Antonia Braithwaite's room the next morning. As the only policeman in Saltings, he would be able to call the case an accident, and tidy up loose ends at his leisure.

At least, he *would* have done – if we had not happened to be there.

This crime did not fit with Mr Victor, who Miss Braithwaite really had disliked immensely. Nor did it fit with her assistant, Miss Singh, who was too small to lift her and too precise to commit such a messy crime, or Mr Geck, who wouldn't have benefited from the unsigned will.

But it did fit with Constable Neaves.

I remembered what Mr Geck had said – that Neaves was new in town. That here, people were more than one thing. A hotel manager could be a bartender. A chambermaid could be a famous swimmer. And a policeman could be a husband, out for revenge.

I thought of what Miss Braithwaite had said the

day before, when she and Mr Victor had argued, and Mr Geck had gone to fetch Neaves from outside to usher Mr Victor away: 'Oh – I can't stand it. He never leaves me alone!' We had thought she meant Mr Victor – but, of course, she meant Neaves.

I looked at him. Would he bluster, or flee? I was not sure he knew, either – but then he gasped and made a grab for the glasses on the chest of drawers. He was trying to destroy the evidence.

'STOP HIM!' shouted Daisy, and we all leaped forward. I got hold of his jacket – and it felt shocking to be laying hold of a policeman in this way. George and Alexander blocked him from touching the glasses, and Neaves gave a furious yell.

'This is ridiculous! This is madness!' Reggie Victor was shouting. Mr Geck was wringing his hands in horror. Only Miss Singh stepped forward.

'Put his cuffs on him,' she said clearly. 'Hurry up and do it. Sam, do you have a room with a lock on it? Some sort of cupboard?'

'There's an empty room on the first floor,' said Mr Geck dizzily. 'I – what—'

'Lock him up there, then,' said Miss Singh. 'Hurry! Reggie, go with him. Go on! I shall call the *real* police.'

'No, wait,' I said. 'Daisy's uncle and aunt – they're out at the moment, but they know important people in the police. They can sort all this out when they get back.'

And that was Neaves done for.

'And to think!' said Daisy that afternoon, once Uncle Felix and Aunt Lucy had returned from their mysterious meeting and called up the Commissioner. The hotel was now swarming with fingerprint experts and police photographers – and all Miss Mottson's friends from the press. 'To think that Uncle Felix and Aunt Lucy wanted to use us as cover for their mission, when *we* were the ones who had the most exciting adventure in the end!'

'I was never enough for her,' Neaves had said bitterly, as he was led away. 'I kept on hoping she'd reconsider – I spent years following her about, trying to get her to see sense. That's why I came here, and why I asked her to meet me. And she agreed, and I thought – at last! But then I saw the will on the side, and realized she was trying to cut me out of her life. I couldn't have that! So I acted.'

'What a silly sob story,' said Daisy, sniffing. 'If only he hadn't already had sleeping drugs in his pocket when he arrived at her room, we might believe it wasn't planned all along. Oh, we ought to be ashamed of ourselves that we didn't tumble to it more quickly, Watson. I've always complained about clodhopping policemen, but I never thought one of them would be a murderer!'

'But really they're only people, just like us,' I said.

'They are *not* just like us,' said Daisy, with dignity. 'We are far better. And aren't we clever! We solved a murder in one morning. We *ought* to get a medal.'

'Tell Uncle Felix,' I said. 'He might give you one.'

'He won't,' said Daisy, sighing. 'He's so boring that way. And I really ought to have solved it more quickly. This murderer was silly and lazy and, well, *clodhopping*. What an idiot!'

'We did solve it, though,' I said, smiling. 'All four of us.'

'*Two* of us!' said Daisy. 'Though I suppose the boys were there as well.'

I felt my face go scarlet.

'Oh, really!' said Daisy. 'Why do you still care about Alexander? You're such a bother, Hazel.'

'I care because he's good, and nice, and . . .

74

sometimes I think he might care about me too,' I said boldly. 'And you can't stop me, Daisy, because I'm *your* bother, and you wouldn't know what to do without me.'

Daisy sighed again. 'It's true,' she said at last. 'I would not want to be without you, no matter how many idiot boys you fall in love with. Now, Hazel, can we *please* go and bathe in the sea?'

I looked outside. A very small spark of sunshine was gilding the edge of a cloud far down on the horizon. And, despite all the horror of the murder, and the shock of its solution, I suddenly felt warm for the first time since we had arrived here in Saltings.

I was with Daisy. We were on holiday. And tomorrow – why, tomorrow was my fifteenth birthday.

'There, see?' said Daisy. 'You look more cheerful already. Didn't I tell you you'd get to like the seaside in the end?'

Acknowledgements

Daisy and Hazel got a World Book Day book! What a dream come true. Thank you to everyone who made it happen, especially booksellers, librarians, teachers and all of my brilliant readers. Huge thanks to the people who gave me feedback to make this story better: L J Moss, James Harkin, Wei Ming Kam and Aishwarya Subramanian, and to Twitter user LifeisGood for Karam's first name. Thanks as always to my publisher Puffin and my amazing Team Bunbreak: Gemma Cooper, Natalie Doherty, Harriet Venn, Sonia Razvi, Nina Tara, Steph Barrett, Jane Tait, Sophie Nelson, Fritha Lindqvist, Ben Hughes and Jasmine Joynson.

Oh, and did you know that the first woman to swim the English Channel was American Gertrude Ederle in 1926, who did it faster than any man had before? GO GERTRUDE!

ACKNOWLEDGEMENTS

UN-*afraid* . . .

UN-*conventional* . . .

UN-*defeated* . . .

UN-*forgettable* . . .

Enter the world of

The UNADOPTABLES

*A magical tale full of fierce
friendship, amazing escapes
and daring adventure . . .*

by Hana Tooke

Illustrated by Ayesha Rubio

COMING MAY 2020

LITTLE TULIP ORPHANAGE, AMSTERDAM, 1880

Little Tulip Orphanage

Rules of Baby Abandonment

RULE ONE: The baby should be wrapped in a cotton blanket.

RULE TWO: The baby should be placed in a wicker basket.

RULE THREE: The baby should be deposited on the topmost step.

In all the years that Elinora Gassbeek had been matron of the Little Tulip Orphanage, not once had the Rules of Baby Abandonment been broken. Until the summer of 1880. Five babies were abandoned at the Little Tulip that autumn and, despite the rules being clearly displayed on the orphanage's front door, not one of these babies was abandoned *sensibly*.

The first baby arrived on a bright morning at the end of August, as dew glistened on the city's cobblestone streets.

Swaddled in a pink cotton blanket, and placed on the appropriate step, was a baby with cocoa-bean eyes and blonde fuzz on its head. However, the way in which Rule Two had been disregarded left no room for forgiveness. The child was snuggled inside a tin toolbox, which had been wrapped with emerald green ribbon, as if it were a present.

'Ugh!' Elinora Gassbeek squawked, looking down at the toolbox-baby in disgust. She signalled a nearby orphan to retrieve it. 'Put it upstairs.'

The orphan nodded. 'What name shall I put on the cot, Matron?'

The matron curled her lip. Naming children was tedious, but necessary.

'She's got a lotta fingers, Matron!'

The baby was sucking its thumb, making loud slurping noises that sent ants crawling up the matron's spine. She counted the child's fingers. Sure enough, it had an extra digit on each hand.

'Name it . . . Lotta.'

The second baby arrived on a blustery evening in September, as a mischievous wind rattled the orphanage's many wooden shutters.

An orphan walked into the dining hall, cradling a coal bucket as if it were a bouquet of flowers. Something was whimpering inside the bucket. Peering in, the matron was displeased to find a raven-haired infant, wrapped in a soot-stained shawl, blinking up at her.

'Poor thing was abandoned beside the coal bunker,' the orphan said.

'Disgraceful!' Gassbeek screeched, referring to the breaking of Rule Two *and* Rule Three. 'Take it away.'

'A name for him, Matron?' the orphan asked nervously.

Elinora Gassbeek took another reluctant look at the coal-bucket baby, its charcoal-blackened nose and the shabby shawl that was wrapped snuggly round it. The cotton shawl looked like it had, possibly, been brightly coloured once. Now, however, it was a mottled shade of grey, with a barely discernible pattern of darker grey ovals. *Like rotten eggs*, the matron thought.

'Name it . . . Egbert.'

The third baby arrived on an unusually warm afternoon in October, as ladies with parasols paraded up and down the sun-warmed street.

Sitting on a bench outside, in her finest puffed-sleeve dress, Elinora Gassbeek opened her picnic hamper and was horrified to find a wriggling baby wedged in among the cheese sandwiches and almond cake. It had a shock of curly red hair and was babbling incessantly.

No cotton blanket. No wicker basket. Not on the topmost step.

The matron screeched shrill and loud like a boiling kettle. The picnic-hamper baby immediately fell silent, its eyebrows squeezing together in a frightened frown. Up and down the street, curious faces appeared in the windows of the tall, narrow brick houses and the strolling ladies came to a halt. Elinora Gassbeek gathered her wits and plastered on a smile for her neighbours. An orphan wove through the throng towards her.

'She wasn't in there a minute ago,' the girl insisted, picking the baby up delicately.

'Take it away,' Elinora Gassbeek said through gritted teeth.

'Yes, Matron. But . . . a name?'

The orphan rocked the now-silent baby, gently brushing fennel seeds from its hair. The matron shuddered.

'Name it . . . Fenna.'

The fourth baby arrived on a gloomy morning in November, as a blanket of fog curled over the canal behind the orphanage.

The delivery bell on the second floor jangled, rung from a boat on the canal below. Using the pulley system attached outside the window, an orphan hoisted the bucket winch up. As it emerged from the fog, Elinora Gassbeek's eye began to twitch. Inside the bucket was a baby wearing a wheat sack and a sad frown. Two holes had been cut in the bottom of the sack to allow its unusually long legs to poke through.

The matron hauled the wheat-sack child inside, cursing the madness that had befallen her orphanage.

'Put some clothes on it,' she cawed to the orphan hovering beside her.

She looked at the baby's wonky ears, its gangly limbs and the wheat-coloured hair that stuck out from its head at the unruliest of angles. Printed on the wheat sack were the words: SEMOLINA FLOUR. The matron groaned.

'Name it . . . Sem.'

The fifth and final baby arrived under a full moon in December, as the constellations shone brightly above Amsterdam's skyline.

Elinora Gassbeek had sent an orphan out on to the Little Tulip's roof to investigate a strange noise. Wedged behind the chimney stack, inside a coffin-shaped basket, was a baby, cooing contentedly up at the starry night sky. It had hair as dark as midnight and eyes that were almost black.

Gingerly, the orphan brought the coffin-basket baby inside, where it immediately began to wail. Careful not to touch the infant, the matron reached down and pulled a toy from its clutches: a cat puppet made from the softest Amsterdam cotton and dressed in fine Antwerp silk. A faint ticking noise emanated from the toy, but the matron was tutting too loudly to hear it.

'Ridiculous!'

She tossed the puppet back in the basket, on top of the black velvet blanket in which the baby was swaddled. On the corner of the blanket, embroidered in white thread, was a name:

Milou.

SHARE A STORY

From breakfast to bedtime, there's always time to discover and share stories together. You can . . .

1 TAKE A TRIP to your LOCAL BOOKSHOP

Brimming with brilliant books and helpful booksellers to share awesome reading recommendations, you can also enjoy booky events with your favourite authors and illustrators.

FIND YOUR LOCAL BOOKSHOP:
booksellers.org.uk/ bookshopsearch

2 JOIN your LOCAL LIBRARY

That wonderful place where the hugest selection of books you could ever want to read awaits – and you can borrow them for FREE! Plus expert advice and fantastic free family reading events.

FIND YOUR LOCAL LIBRARY:
gov.uk/local-library-services/

3 CHECK OUT the WORLD BOOK DAY WEBSITE

Looking for reading tips, advice and inspiration? There is so much for you to discover at **worldbookday.com**, packed with fun activities, games, downloads, podcasts, videos, competitions and all the latest new books galore.

SPONSORED BY
NATIONAL BOOK tokens

Rob Biddulph

Celebrate stories. Love reading.

World Book Day is a registered charity funded by publishers and booksellers in the UK & Ireland.

Well **hello** there! We are

Overjoyed that you have **joined our celebration** of

Reading **books** and **sharing stories**, because we

Love bringing **books** to you.

Did you know, we are a **charity** dedicated to celebrating the

Brilliance of **reading for pleasure** for everyone, everywhere?

Our mission is to help you discover **brand new stories** and

Open your mind to exciting **new worlds** and **characters**, from

Kings and **queens** to **wizards** and **pirates** to **animals** and **adventurers** and so many more. We couldn't

Do it without all the amazing **authors** and **illustrators**, **booksellers** and **bookshops**, **publishers**, **schools** and **libraries** out there –

And most importantly, we couldn't do it all without . . .

YOU!

On your bookmarks, get set. READ!
Happy Reading. Happy World Book Day.

ILLUSTRATOR *Rob Biddulph*